RESCUING THE VEXATIOUS BOSS

IN THE THROES OF LOVE

BY

JAYLANI ANGELIQUE

DISCLAIMER

This book is rated 18+ as it contains erotic content not suitable for a child below the specified age.

TABLE OF CONTENTS

Grab a Cup of Coffee, Relax and Enjoy

the Story.

It's time to escape the Reality!

CHAPTER ONE

KNOCKING ON DEATH'S DOOR

D ave you have to come home," Dave Anderson turned off the tread mill, pulled the towel hanging around his neck and wiped the sweat trailing down a chin that had grown a morning stumble, his well muscled body which had been a result of regular exercise and playing football during his college days, was sleek with sweat. He threaded his long fingers through his midnight dark hair as he stepped down from the exercising machine to listen to what Mark had to say. Something was wrong. "What's going on Mark?" he asked gruffly. He hoped this was not another ploy to get him home. He hadn't been to his parent's home in Washington for months with an excuse that he'd been extremely busy. He truly was, but he could have made time to visit them in the last six months, but he hadn't. He was trying to avoid his father's bullying and his mom's nagging. Not to misunderstand him, he loved his parents to boot, but when you are an only son at the age of thirty seven without any inclination of getting married in the closest future, your parents would definitely hold a noose around your neck. "It's your dad." Mark Smith was David Anderson's Lawyer/ closest advisor/ friend. Those two were as thick as thieves. Dave's father had never involved his friend in any of his schemes before. His father must be getting desperate. "Whatever it is, tell him I'm not interested, I'm certain this is another trick to get me home and take over the seat of the CEO." He paused for effect. "Meredith is very much interested in taking over the company, I'm not the only child, plus she is the first-born, remember?"

Dave had never made it a secret that he was in no way interested in taking any claim to his father's company; Leaver Land Company. He had his own French wine and spirit producing company which he had built from the scratch five years ago. Sterling company was fast growing into a multimillion enterprise and he had more than his hands full running the company, with the help of his employees of course.

Being on the list of top ten most eligible bachelors in the state had made him a foremost target for women; however he wasn't 'settling down' and producing little Andersons anytime time soon, much to his parent's despair. He was a boss who commanded respect and didn't give laxity or excuses when it comes to completing a task. Many had deemed him an extreme workaholic and a domineering asshole; however, his close friends knew he played hard just as he worked hard. Dave was not one to shirk his duties, but taking on the position as the CEO at his father's company would not only put a strain on him, but it would also be unnecessary since Meredith and a couple of board members could take over the post. She currently owns a large share of the company as a part of her inheritance and she was also an administrator at the company. Although Dave wasn't fond of his sister for some obvious reasons, but he had to admit she was very good at her job. More like a machine and Dave knew she would be more than ecstatic to be given the post as the CEO. But for some reason, his father had insisted on enforcing the post on him, claiming the rest of the board wouldn't accept Meredith because she is female and he doesn't want some stranger running his own company when he had a living son. It all sounded terribly archaic to his hearing. "This is no ploy, it's very serious in fact, your Dad had a cardiac arrest and he's been rushed to the hospital."

His nerves plummeted, that couldn't be true, the old devil still called him the other night threatening to cut him off his inheritance if he didn't come home to do what he deemed the needful. Of course it couldn't be true. Dave gained some equilibrium and his nerves quickly settled. "Nice try Mark, nice try." He said repeated, chuckling. "I thought mum would be the one to pull this up, not that.... Thought the old bull was too prideful to feign ill health." He snickered as he fixed his ear pod properly in his left ear. An exasperated sigh reached him from the ear pod. "I called because your father is in no condition to do so, and I know how much you'd hate it if you weren't there for your father, this might be it." Mark stated soberly. 'Wait a minute, it might actually be true', Dave thought, is father actually dying? It was too difficult wrapping his head around it.

"I'm taking the first flight." He stated with urgency.

"I already sent a chopper to pick you up." Mark informed.

One of the quacks of being filthy rich is that you can get anything or do anything at your convenience. He wasn't one of those who felt guilty about spending money, albeit lavishly. He believes you shouldn't deny yourself of things you desire if you can get them and that includes women also, and he has those in spades, in fact they usually fall over themselves just to have him.

He didn't bother packing a bag; he knew everything he might need would be arranged by his personal assistant, Cynthia Campbell; she was very diligent and efficient at her job. He already notified her and she set things into motion. About fifteen minutes after he got into the chopper, they were almost landing at their destination. Dave suddenly felt a pang in his chest, like his heart was being pulled, he took in deep breaths and took a sip of the bottled water beside his armrest. Something was definitely wrong. Immediately as he landed at the airport, a Mercedes was already parked in waiting with the driver standing right beside it. He walked hurriedly towards it in long strides. The driver quickly opened the passenger's door to let him in. He immediately got in, He dialed his mother's line, but she wasn't picking up, called Mark, he wasn't reachable. And the last person he could think of calling was Meredith. Nevertheless, he did.

The phone rang twice, and she picked on the forth ring. "How's Dad?' He asked gruffly, no point dallying around and asking about her welfare when she'd only throw insults at him.

"It's a fine day for you to finally call, after living for months without looking back." Meredith snapped.

"I just want to know about Dad's condition; I trust you are at the hospital already."

"If you want to know about his condition, come see him for yourself." She said waspishly and ended the call.

It never fails to nettle him anytime he and his sister communicate; its why he usually avoids any contact with her. He couldn't recall the last time he and his sister were cordial towards each other. Although, he vaguely remembered that she used to laugh and play with him when they were kids. He wondered why and when it all changed. Actually if he should be honest with himself, he knew the answer to those questions. She was two years older than him at the age of thirty nine. There was this stiffness that was always there. It seemed she resented his very existence and it actually got worse after she got married to her douche bag of a husband; Paul. It's not like he cared anyways. The only good thing that came out of their union was his sixteen year old niece named Lucy, how those two could birth such a gorgeous kind hearted girl was totally beyond him.

He was jostled back into the present when the car's engine was turned off immediately once they got to the hospital. He stepped out of the car and his long legs ate up the ground until he got to the waiting area where he was greeted with Paul's assessing gaze and his sister's cold attitude. His mum was seated, looking totally miserable. You couldn't catch Sarah Anderson dead looking anything but perfect, her hair was never out of place and her dressing style was impeccable, Meredith took after her in that, the only difference was that his mother was warm hearted while Meredith was as cold as death.

He sat beside his mother and put a comforting arm around her; she immediately went into his arms and sobbed like her heart was being torn out. He rested his chin on the top of her head with his eyes closed wishing he could take her pain away. "Could you walk into the office with me Mr. Anderson?" A gray haired man dressed in scrubs addressed soberly addressed him.

He was the family's doctor Paddy McLain and he had been for years.

"I'm coming with him." Meredith perked up behind him.

"I'd advice you take your mother home instead." Doctor McLain suggested. "Your brother would relay the conclusions to you." The doctor added.

Meredith looked like she would rather stay right there and insist to be let in on whatever was going to be discussed. It seemed she thought better of it and decided to listen to the doctor. This strange because Meredith rarely listened to anyone except herself. "Let's go home mum." She said gently to her mother. "Home? Where?" Sarah asked with a bewildered expression. "Home at Collin Way mum," Meredith responded gently, looking confused. Dave would have probably been concerned, but the poor woman had been through a lot, it's no surprise her mind was a bit jumbled at the moment.

"Home mum," Dave added.

"Oh, right...home." She sighed as if finally getting where they where referring to. "But I'd rather wait till your father wakes up, I don't want to leave." Their mother insisted stubbornly, pursing her lips.

"There is nothing you can do for him now Mrs. Anderson, You wouldn't be helping if you fall ill yourself." The doctor advised. "He's already stabilized and I know he'll be fine." The doctor reassured the poor woman.

"Remember that he would believe the apocalypse has occurred if he sees you looking like this." Dave teased, which finally got her into motion and she stood up.

"Alright love, Meredith let's go, I should go freshen up for my husband." She tittered as they walked out the doorway with Paul. The bastard hadn't even let out a single word.

Dave wondered why he showed up any way. His dad had never liked him one bit. Daniel wouldn't have allowed Paul to marry his only daughter if stubborn Meredith hadn't insisted on it. He knew down to his bones Paul only married his sister because of their father's wealth, the sneaky bastard. Immediately they were out of sight, Doctor Mclain walked him to his office, and gestured for him to sit.

"I want to see my father." Dave stated immediately.

"Of course," the doctor responded and led him to the ward where his father laid. He felt like he'd been sucker punched when he saw the frail looking man who couldn't possibly be his father on the hospital bed. Daniel Anderson wasn't so tall like his son, but he'd always seemed larger than life with his indomitable presence. He commanded respect whenever he entered an arena. It hurt him to see his father looking so lifeless on the hospital bed. He wasn't aware the doctor had left to give them room for privacy; he slowly walked to his father's bed and held his thin bloodless hands. He was hooked up to medical equipment and an intravenous device. A nasal canola was attached to his nose to pass oxygen into his lungs. His father looked a hundred years older.

It seemed like his father felt his presence and his eyes slowly flickered open. Dave was already lost in his misery as he tearfully held his father's hands, he wasn't aware his father was already awake. "If I had known it would take a heart attack to get you home, I'd have had one a long time ago," a gruff voice that is badly in need of water uttered croakily. Dave immediately jerked his head upward to look into familiar seafoam green eyes, eyes that were just like his. The relief he felt at the sound of his father's voice almost knocked him to his knees, he wasn't ready to lose him just yet. "I knew you were feigning it, the shows over... just know you wouldn't get me to sign that piece of paper you've been hounding me to sign." He joked. Of course he knew the heart attack was serious, no one could feign being this bloodless, he was just so glad to have his father back that he couldn't help needling him a bit.

"You wouldn't accept even if I died?" His father asked gruffly, with a feeble quirk to his lips.

The smile of Dave's face quickly dropped at his father's words. 'Don't joke about things like that, Dad." Dave retorted sternly, albeit gently. It wouldn't do to get annoyed with the pigheaded man at the moment.

"When are you given me some grandbabies then?"

His father was probably the only man who could be on a sick bed and still have the capability to harass you.

"Meredith already gave you a beautiful granddaughter dad." Dave responded in exasperation.

"Of course, my grandbaby is a huge gift to me, at least that's a compensation for adding that slime of a man to the family." Daniel added in annoyance. "But I haven't gotten any from you." He insisted looking pointedly at his son. "You know I would have loved to see them before I died." His father added.

Dave didn't like that tone a single bit. "You ain't going anywhere dad, if you want to see your precious grandkids, you've got to stay alive." He said good-naturedly, but he meant every word. He couldn't imagine his father dying just yet. The old bull was too stubborn to give up that easily anyway.

"I'm glad you came, son." His father murmured with a wealth of meaning behind those words.

"Of course I would, even if it only to needle you back to good health." Dave stated, with humor back in his voice.

"I love you son."

'I love you too dad."

"Now, I'm just going to sleep for a bit." His father said beneath his breath as his eyes began flickering close just as the monitor began beeping noisily. Something was wrong. Dave immediately ran out to call for the doctor, anyone who could help. The doctor and two nurses quickly dashed into the ward, placed his stethoscope on Daniels chest and tried regulating his breathing. A nurse quickly ushered Dave out of the room, but he was too stubborn to budge. The monitor suddenly let of a flat sound and his father's breathing stopped.

Dave's back hit the wall as he realized his father was dead.

CHAPTER TWO

WHAT A DAY!

hat a shitty day' Leila Brandon thought angrily as she slammed the door of her room shut, waking her roommate/ sister/best friend from her afternoon nap.

"Leila, what the heck!" she growled as she stumbled awake, rising reluctantly from the couch. Leila didn't respond, she simply slumped down on the couch beside her sister-friend with a 'woe is me' look.

"What happened this time?" Kendra asked tiredly, sweeping her long blond hair backwards, away from her face. She might be concerned, but she looked like she'd rather go back to sleep and knowing Leila, she wasn't getting a wink of sleep until she gets off whatever she has on her mind.

"Can you believe that shitty, nincompoop, asshole……" she trailed off when she ran out of insults, she was so worked up her chest was heaving.

"Okay, okay, I get it." Kendra said gently, she really was exhausted from her nights shift.

"Can you believe he laid me off because of because of some huge boobs?" Leila spat indignantly.

"Wait; hold on… huge boobs came for the interview, as in walking boobs." Kendra asked with eyes as wide as saucers and Leila gave her a look that said she thought she was dim witted.

"You said boobs didn't you?" She wondered aloud.

"Why are you being deliberately obtuse, you know that wasn't what I meant." She spat indignantly.

"Sorry, you know I'm not usually so clear headed until I get a glass of water," she said apologetically as she walked toward the kitchen to get herself some water.

"Everything was going just fine, I had passed the whole exercise, until the physical interview, all the blond bimbo had to do was waltz past the randy goat and he was dancing to her tune. I'd bet my last cash that she knows little about business management." She added angrily as if she hadn't stopped speaking earlier.

"You really need to stop speaking in parables or is it idioms?"

'This really isn't the time Kendra." Leila stated as her fury gave way to exasperation.

"Didn't I tell you to loosen up a few buttons earlier this morning before stepping out the door?" She questioned lightly as Leila turned red.

"I wouldn't prostitute myself just because I need a job. If any guy boss is stupid enough not to see how smart I am, then it's his loss." She said waspishly.

Kendra studied her friend with a clear gaze, taking in the button down army green shirt which did little to enhance her already beautiful olive skin, at least her pencil skirt fit snuggly to her rounded hips, and it sort of complimented the billowy shirt and not a single perch of skin as revealed. It seemed Leila intentionally goes all the way to cover up herself. Kelly took a look at her friends face and saw not a stitch of makeup in sight except for the clear gloss, which was only applied because her lips were dry. Her long darkest brown hair was pulled back severely into a tight bun. In all, her friend was gorgeous, but she currently looked like someone's governess. "What's with the long assessment?" Leila bristled, already guessing what her friend was about to say, however she was surprised.

"You are gorgeous you know, I'm talking drop dead gorgeous and I'd kill to have skin, ass and boobs like yours." Kendra surmised wishfully. Leila was full breasted. "Only if you could wear the right clothing, you'd knock 'em off their socks."

"I believe it's 'heels' not 'socks'". Leila corrected with a snort.

Rolling her eyes, Kendra said, "whatever, as long as you get my meaning." Without pausing, she added, "I know you're very smart. In fact, if you ask me, I'd say you are exceptionally intelligent. I'm not saying this because you are my sister and best friend, but because I know you're freakishly brilliant, but upping your game by dressing cool and sexy doesn't make you a slut." "I like my clothes." Leila argued.

"Most of them belong in the not so trendy styles of the '90s" Kendra retorted. Anyway, I know you'll get another job soon. Some lucky industry will see just how amazing your brain works and will sweep you right in." She added, tapping her friends lap encouragingly.

'It's not like you're so stranded that you need a job ASAP, all you have to do is call daddy dearest." Kendra quipped as Leila quirked her lips.

It was a nick name Kendra calls their father, Matt Brandon. He was a kind hearted man who had unofficially adopted the newly orphaned Kendra, whose parents had died in a ghastly accident and Leila, also an orphan and welcomed them into his small family with open arms. After all, what's one or two more daughters when he wanted a full house? Matt was a distinguished lecturer at Brainerd University, he was well off and he could provide adequately for his family. If it were up to him, he would have Leila and Kendra living with him. But the girls had insisted on staying on their own and giving him and his newly wedded wife, Miriam, some "privacy". "I'm not asking dad for money when I'm perfectly capable of taking care of myself." Kendra snorted, "Of course you are."

"And what's that supposed to mean?" Leila asked, looking ready to pounce.

"Nothing." Kendra said as she went into the kitchen search of something to eat and also avoiding her pig headed sister-friend's wrath. Promising herself that someday, she's going to burn those horrible clothes.

"So what was the opening you were telling me about yesterday?" Leila questioned as Kendra returned from the kitchen.

"Oh, I thought you weren't interested since it was an opening for an intern." Kendra responded from the kitchen at the top of her voice. 'I never said I wasn't interested, did I?" she asked. "I'd just prefer to get staffed than work as an intern at that company." She added wistfully.

"Do you know that Leaver Land is one of the largest manufacturing companies in the Washington state area, with branches within and outside the state, New York in particular? If you asked me, I'd have said you should give the internship a shot and you could be staffed afterwards, which I know you would." Kendra stated reasonably.

"Alright" she stated, giving in.

Leila and Kendra had both rounded up with college about half a year ago, Kendra had been content working as a bartender at one of the renowned gentleman's clubs in the city, while Leila had insisted on looking for a more 'lucrative job', nevertheless, she waitresses at the same club Kendra works at. It wasn't strenuous and it was fun, however she planned on suspending the fun and resigning once she had gotten what she wanted.

"How did you get the info anyway?" Leila couldn't help but ask.

"One of the perks of working as a bartender at a classy men's club. Plus…" Kendra ended with a deliberate pause, which Leila knew would be an intro for a not so subtle insult. 'There's something called the internet you know?" she added, with a tease.

CHAPTER THREE

TESTING DANGEROUS WATERS

I t's been a week since Dave's father was laid to rest, and he felt like he had left a huge void in Dave's heart. If anyone had told him he'd miss that pig headed old man that much, he might have snorted. Days ago, Dave found it difficult at accept the demise of his father. Daniel Anderson had seemed so invisible and he had been one of those people whom you think would live forever.

"So, are you taking on the post of the CEO at your father's company?' Brad, his best friend all the way back to college days-asked him as he took a sip of wine.

"I haven't made up my mind yet," Dave responded honestly, he might change some things, but whatever he did, he'd be trusting his instincts.

They were currently lounging at a VIP section in a renowned gentleman's club in Washington, Brad had driven all the way from New York to attend and pay his last respect to a man who was a force to be reckoned with and to also grant his best friend some moral support during the funeral. He had decided to stay the rest of the week just to relax a bit before resuming at his own company. Brad was from a family popularly classified as those with old money; however he was a notorious womanizer and was unrepentant about it.

The two friends didn't talk much after that, they simply took in their environment as music boomed around them and extremely beautiful waitresses strutted around in uniforms that did little to cover their skins. A couple of waitresses who had attended to them had flirted outrageously with them, but Dave granted them no audience, however Brad was just too happy to oblige.

A dark brunette dressed in a similar outfit but with less skin revealed suddenly walked past their seat to another section without a single glance in their direction. Dave's attention was drawn to her as he studied her beneath deep-set eyes. She was dressed in tight leather skirt that fell just above are knees, a white button down shirt was tied to a knot right on her belly, but not above her navel like the rest. She screamed conservative and do not touch. But Dave was tempted to do exactly that. The oblivious brunette went on her business without noticing someone's gaze tracing her every step, until finally, she felt a pricking of a gaze and she stopped mid step with a tray of drinks in hand and turned towards the direction of the gaze. Her eyes clashed with heated green eyes that seemed to hold her immobile. She couldn't move an inch until a guy who was tipsy crashed into her, causing some drinks to spill on her shirt.

She quickly recovered her consciousness, apologizing profusely to the person who crashed into her thinking she was at fault, her mind was that befuddled.

Dave already had a stern scowl on his face at the scene that unfolded before him. He was half tempted to go to her and punch the idiot who had stumbled into her, but he quickly stopped and brought his emotions under control. When had he ever felt such a protective instinct for someone who wasn't even a close relative? Thank God she wasn't. Whatever he felt for her was anything but familial. He would have left Brad there after a couple of drinks, his friend was too occupied with a somewhat busty blonde to want to leave anytime soon, and even if he would, there weren't heading to the same destination and he had no desire to be a third wheel. He silently kept track of the little brunette that had caught his unwavering attention. He couldn't remember the last time he felt so excited about anything until tonight, he wanted her, and he was definitely having her that night.

The club was still bustling, although it was already late into the night. He noticed the brunette had disappeared for a while, he didn't understand the sheer panic he almost felt at the thought that she might have left. But his mind was laid to rest again when he recollected that he had already tipped some of the bouncers to keep an eye on her. He would have been informed if she had left. Within minutes he saw her high tail towards the door, dressed in baggy shorts and billowy t-shirt that did little to hide her rack even from this distance. Her appearance only fascinated Dave and he desired to pill off every shred of clothing to unveil what would sure be breathtaking gifts that lay beneath them.

******

It had been a hectic night, which only got worse after she crashed into the poor tipsy guy. Thankfully her shift was finally over and all she wanted to do was marry her bed all through the night with zero disturbance. Also, there's that interview she had again. She groaned inwardly at the thought. Surprisingly, she wasn't really tired, not as tired as she usually felt most nights, but it seemed she been strangely electrified and simultaneously energized by the locked gaze she had shared with the hot green eyed stranger. She suddenly felt heated all over on remembering the earlier incident. As she was about to slide out the entrance of the VIP section, Peter; a tall brawny bouncer who had no business being named after a biblical paragon blocked her exit. He was a terribly sweet guy despite his huge built, but he was a relentless womanizer.

"Leila, you leaving already?" He questioned with a grin that must have dropped many panties but not hers.

"Yep, my shifts over, is there something I'm needed for?" Leila asked him with a raised brow.

"Uhmmm, Dave Anderson wants to meet you." He answered with his grin still in place; it only seemed a bit wider.

"Sorry, I don't have time for that." Leila stated hurried as she made a move towards the door, but the shocked look on Peter's face stopped her.

"Why is your mouth gapping open, flies could perch in if you're not careful," She teased.

"Don't you know who he is?"

"I can't keep track of the name of everyone who steps into this club." She stated waspishly.

"You are actually leaving?" Peter's question in bare concealed amazement.

"Yeah, watch me." Leila retorted cheekily as she stepped a foot out.

What's the harm in staying to share a couple of drinks with a really hot guy, moreover it's been a while since she had had actual fun. Having a change of heart, she whirled around and faced Peter.

"The management wouldn't like it." She objected tentatively.

"The management wouldn't say shit" Peter reassured with a rakish smile. "Hasn't your friend had a thousand hook ups here after her shift, did you see anyone raising an alarm?" He questioned reasonably, referring to Kendra. "As long as it isn't affecting your job, you'll be fine. Moreover, where is your friend, she should be the one giving this speech, not me." He added jokingly.

Having seemed to be reassured by Peter's words, she took in a deep breath, conceded and walked towards the 'Dave Anderson'. Her sneakers encased legs almost became shaky as she moved closer to him, Gawd, he was hot! The other blond haired Adonis sitting beside him earlier had suddenly disappeared and he was currently the only one occupying the space. She took in his appearance even as she walked closer, he had thick black hair that looked like he or someone had run fingers through the mane, and she was tempted to do just that, a hawk-like nose that almost seemed too big for his face, but the imperfection only added to his uniqueness, he had lips that looked like they were made for sexual purposes alone. The upper lip was slightly fuller that the lower; they were wide and bow shaped, and looked like the only soft feature out of his iron carved looks. She finally took in the eyes and she felt like she'd been sucker punched by a trailer. They were simply beautiful. His heavily lidded, deep set green eyes were reciprocating the same thorough examination she had been carrying out on him, but whatever he might be feeling was concealed beneath them.

He sat up straighter and moved a bit to create some space for her to sit. "I usually don't this you know? I don't hang at my work place." Leila objected half heartedly, she didn't get the reason she felt the need to say that.

"I wasn't aware there was and hanging section in here." A gruff voice teased jokingly.

She simply shrugged as her confidence began to wane a bit. This guy was seriously sucking her in with his dominating aura, he screamed power and money. Those weren't the reasons why she was so intrigued by him, but there was just something about him that she couldn't resist.

"My name is Dave." He added.

She debated for a minute about making up a name, but she quickly dismissed it, there were a thousand Leila's anyway. "Mine's Leila."

For once, she decided to let go and have some fun. And she did, immediately her mind was made up, she became more relaxed and they their conversation varied from the littlest things to the important things, but they never discussed details about their family. It turned out she had some real fun, although, she had gotten a little tipsy. To be honest, she was more than a little tipsy, but she wasn't seeing in two's yet so she was still okay. It'd been so long since she had enjoyed a male's company, not for the lack of attention but because she just wasn't interested.

"I think I should leave now." She said reluctantly.

"I'll drive you." He offered not giving her a chance to say no. she was about to do just that, but her refusal died on her lips when she saw how determined he was, rising to his feet and helping her up on hers. They both walked out the noisy club into the somewhat cold night.

They moved toward a black Benz parked just at the corner of the parking lot, when they got there, he moved to open the door for her to get in, she moved to do just that when he suddenly held her left arm, and turned her to face his deep set eyes It was dark, but those green eyes were clearly flashing with unbridled desire.

"I'm going to kiss you." He half stated and half asked. The answer was right there in her eyes, in the slight opening of her lips and her shortened breath. She wanted the kiss just as much as he did.

He pulled her to his chest and laid his lips in hers, he gently probed her with his tongue to open up, and immediately she did, he swept in and kissed her like a drowning man. She reciprocated with the same fervor until she felt like she couldn't breathe. His hands started trailing a swift route all over her body, her t shirt was already deftly loosed and she suddenly felt his palms on her bare skin. She jerked with desire and it felt like he was branding her wherever his hand laid. She couldn't take anymore, the assault was too much on her senses and she broke the heated kiss. He looked like he'd been jerked back to earth also as he delved his hands into his hair and fought for a control he'd never had a reason to lose. He had to have her now.

"My place," he stated, imploring her with hungry eyes to give in and for the second time in a row, she threw caution to the wind and nodded. It was certainly a night she would never forget.

CHAPTER FOUR

WALK OF SHAME

L eila rubbed her swollen eyes as her inner alarm bells sent her

awake. Why did it fill like she had run a marathon all through the

night? She felt very, but deliciously tired, she was sore in places

she never knew existed. Why did everything seem so foggy? She

held her hand to her clamming forehead, why did it feel like a pack of elephants had battled on her head, it was pounding. She looked downward at the blanket that covered her and realized this wasn't her familiar penguin blanket. What's going on? She wondered. She looked beneath the blanket and saw she was stark naked. A heavy limb that certainly wasn't hers suddenly fell on her thigh; she jerked her head to view the face attached to the arm and saw the handsome devil she had spent the night with. Everything came flooding back, she could recollect everything and all that they had done all through the night, her cheeks got flushed on remembering the wicked things he had done to her and the uninhibited manner she had responded to his touches. It was wonderful. His eyes suddenly got as wide as saucers when she recalled the interview she had that morning. She gently moved so as not to wake him and got of the bed. She cringed at the prospect of carrying out her walk of shame and hoped he wouldn't come awake until she leaves. Luckily, he didn't until she finished throwing on her clothes, she couldn't find her panties, they were probably strewn somewhere. She walked to the door and allowed herself one last look before walking out and shutting the door gently behind her.

It was already 8:30 am by the time she got home. On getting there, Leila knew Kendra was around and she had actually wished she would stay longer at her boyfriend's place. She didn't want Kendra catching her doing her walk of shame. She tip toed into the house, so Kendra wouldn't hear her walk in. she was probably still sleeping. She almost got past the living room when she heard the familiar impish voice say, "Look what the cat dragged in." Leila comically stopped on her tracks and looked upward in exasperation. 'You know I actually prayed that you wouldn't be home." Leila stated unrepentantly, taking a peek at her sister-friend's face.

"No need to look all guilty, you're not underage, are you?" she teased."I can't believe you finally got the cobwebs down there cleared off." She added with a whoop and Leila hoped the whole neighborhood didn't her obnoxious announcement.

"Who was he? No. wait – wait, was it good?' Kendra continued, quirking her brows. This was one on the moments Leila wished she had a gag in hand.

Leila simply shook her head irritated, knowing there was no way she could get her nosey sister-friend to either butt out nor shut up, she was like a dog with a bone.

"Come on tell me, I want every juicy detail." She insisted which only increased Leila's annoyance.

"Kendra, I'm late for an interview." She snapped.

It seemed to have taken Kendra some time to process Leila's announcement, then she suddenly cursed, 'Oh shit!"

*****

Immediately Dave walked into Leaver Land conference room, the whole place quieted, it obvious they had already begun the meeting in his absence, which was not their fault since he'd arrived forty five minutes later than the time scheduled for the meeting. He had such a great night, so great that he'd over slept. Overslept! Something he didn't think would ever happen to him. He was a stickler for time, but it was worth it, the memory almost brought a smile to his face, but it was immediately wiped off when he remembered he had woken up to a cold bed. She had run away.

That was something he had never dreamed would happen to him. He had always been the one sending them away, not the other way round. And he could bet his entire fortune that she had enjoyed the night as much as he did if the claw marks on his chest and back he had saw in the mirror had been any indication. So why the hell did she run away?

"Mr. Anderson... Mr. Anderson?" One of the board members called his name incessantly.

He quickly recollected his thoughts and brought his mind back to the present.

"Yes, I will be acting as the new CEO and after a few months will be fully appointed as the CEO of the company according to the management's regulations." He announced. There were thirteen members of the committee seated round the desk which included his sister and her husband; the slimy bastard did luck out marrying Meredith. Mark was also present.

Some of those seated looked like they agreed with him, which wasn't surprising since he already managed and owned a thriving enterprise of his own, so his capabilities couldn't be doubted. However, there were some members who looked like they opposed his speech and would very much prefer he didn't emerge as the CEO. That group of people clearly belongs to Meredith and her husband's caucus.

Just to be clear, aside from the fact that him becoming the CEO was his father's dying wish, the major reason he accepted the post was because he didn't want his sibling getting that post because she was almost as capable as him. If she does become the CEO, her husband will have more leeway for the already suspicious activity and business deals he had been undertaking with the companies name, and if not careful, he will run it to the ground. So you see, Dave just had to take it up. Aside from him, the very few he could have nominated for the position were also capable, but he remembered it was his dad who had always been against an outsider taking over his company. The opinion was probably archaic, but he wants to keep his late father's wishes. 'The company needs someone who would dedicate a hundred percent attention to it." Paul stated calmly and that voice really irked Dave.

"And what makes you think I'd be distracted or I wouldn't be capable of running both companies?" Dave asked with a deadly calm, everyone might be fooled, but not Meredith... she knew her brother was getting furious. The idiot had the nerve to converse with him directly, he's definitely grown wings now that Daniel was no more. Dave suspected he must have graduated to a higher level in executing the shady deals he within the company.

"According to the deceased will, Mr. Anderson is entitled to the position, although it is subject to the board's approval, if he carried out his duties efficiently as the Chief Executive Manager." Mark explains.

"And if he doesn't?"This came from Steve, a male executive in his forties which had been dedicated to the company according to the records shown. He hadn't stayed clearly on whose side he was, maybe he was choosing now.

"Someone else would be voted in for the position." Meredith supplied with a good dose of pleasure.

'This is totally hilarious". Dave thought.

"You are all aware I do have my own company, Sterling and it's a successful one, so I'm not here for whatever ulterior motive some of you might be thinking about. And again, I'm only taking this up because it's a duty and I'm taking it as such. So pending the time I'm here, even if you vote me in or out, there's going to be a lot of changes going on. So put on your seat belts." He added with a shit eating grin. Some bastards were going to lose their minds or… their jobs. "So, you're welcome on board Dave." Louis congratulated Dave with a handshake and so did others, except his sister's caucus of course.

Turning to face Paul, Dave asked, "I want the reports on the previous finances." Without breaking the eye contact, Paul responded, "Sure."

The board members dispersed, each going to their various destinations. However, Dave had decided to wait a bit so he could do some checking on the company. From what he'd seen, the company should be earning twice the amount coming in. Although truth be told, the company is not suffering due to any monetary loss. Nevertheless, it should be more. He sat on the comfy executive seat in father's office, which he now occupies since he'd been selected as the acting CEO. He was certain the old man was probably barking out in laughter that he finally gave in to what he wanted him to do. He had been poring through file upon files all day. He was almost through checking and he still hadn't found any sign of abnormality in the companies finances.

He looked up to see it was almost midnight, he knew he had taking a lot of time and he was prepared for it. He finally decided to give it a rest and return to his condominium in Seattle Washington. At the thought, his mind drifted back to the not so mysterious Leila. He could find her if he wanted to, the truth was he really wanted to, but he wasn't one to allow his emotions rule him. He realized his thoughts had been so preoccupied with her that he hadn't felt that pang in his chest whenever he recollected that his father was dead.

He looked around the office and saw his father's imprints, the hideous art work gotten by Daniel still hung on the left side of the wall, a picture of Sarah, Meredith, Lucy and him was still positioned on the desk. For all the old guy's stubbornness and commanding attitude, he loved his family dearly. It hurt Dave so much that he was gone.

His mind drifted worriedly to his mother, who had been acting strangely since his father's death; she forgot things a lot and sometimes spoke out of context. At first he had chalked it all up to grieving Daniel's death, but as time went on, they realized it was more than that.. Just two days ago when he had gone to visit her, she had asked him about his training section, he hadn't trained for football since college. He didn't want to get alarmed, but he was worried something was terribly wrong. He just hoped that whatever it is shouldn't be terrible and his mum could return to her healthy normal self. Thankfully, she had been to the hospital for some examinations, whatever the problem was, he was getting to the bottom of it. He'd just lost a father and he wasn't going to lose his mother too.

CHAPTER FIVE

TOTALLY UNEXPECTED

rs. Anderson has been diagnosed with Alzheimer's disease; "it's a form of dementia." Doctor McLain explained.

"So are you saying she's going crazy?' Meredith asked, perplexed.

"Of course she's not." Dave retorted.

"There's no reason to panic, this occurs in aged men and women and I guess losing your father also contributed to it." The doctor explained. "But you do not need to be alarmed, it can be managed." Doctor McLain added.

"I don't want it managed, I want it cured." Dave spat. The four walls of the doctor's office already felt like they were closing in on him. He thought he was prepared for whatever the problem was, but he certainly wasn't expecting dementia, a disease that could well reduce the strongest of men into raving lunatics. This couldn't possibly happen to his mother.

"Sadly, there's no cure for dementia at the moment, but the good news is that it can be managed. I'd refer you to a specialist who would give you further information on what to do. And trust me; Mrs. Anderson would be in good hands." He stated calmly, with a little attempt at smiling. There was actually nothing to smile about.

"Thank you Doctor", Meredith said and she stood and walked out of the office without waiting for Dave to follow.

Immediately once they got outside and away from the hospital vehicles and walked out under the heated sun towards the parking lot, Dave called her name, "Meredith".

She stopped immediately, but it took her a second to turn around, and when she did, the scowl on her face was a strong indication that she was in no mood to entertain whatever thoughts he had to share. "We need to talk." He stated neutrally.

"I don't think so." She responded tonelessly. "Will you listen to reason for a minute?" He gritted out between clenched teeth. His sister could tempt a saint. He looked hard to the honey colored eyes balls that where so like his mother, he tried to search for some warmth there, but all he saw was absolute resistance.

"Okay fine, get it out." She conceded after debating within herself.

"Mom can't stay alone"

"She isn't." She supplied tonelessly. "Willow and the rest of the housekeeping staff are with her." She added.

"I can't believe this, sometimes, I wonder how and when you turned into such a cold bitch." He growled. Meredith didn't even blink at the insult; she only studied him beneath her gaze like a yapping puppy who was simply an annoyance.

"If stating plain facts makes me a bitch, I wonder what that would make you." Meredith retorted flatly without an ounce of emotion.

"Mum needs to be around family."

"We are within driving distance aren't we? Listen, I know you are concerned about her and whether you believe it or not, I am also and she is my mother." She said calmly. "For now, she isn't acting weirdly out of context yet and according to the doctor, the condition can be managed. And as far as I am concerned, Willow is family. So mother will be fine." She reassured.

Dave had to blink twice to double check if the person speaking was his older sister, as it was the first time in years she had spoken so civilly towards him. What was up with her?

"If that'll be all, I'd like to be on my way." She turned without saying good bye and sashayed away.

***

"The boss requested you see him in his office," Bianca Stone informed her tonelessly. She was a gorgeous blond bombshell, who seemed to have zero fat, a perfect face and an equally perfect body which was always encased in penciled skirts and peekaboo toed, heeled shoes. She was in charge of supervising the interns, and was also the biggest of all bitches within the company's walls, though maybe just in their work space. It actually wasn't fair that mean women get to look so breath taking, life could be so ironic. Leila could never understand why Bianca had taken such a strong dislike to her. Fine she might not be a social person, but she had gotten along with everyone at her work space except her, and she was her direct boss, Leila hoped with all her heart Bianca wouldn't cause her undue stress.

"Alright, should I take along the document you wanted me to give him earlier?" Leila asked. "You aren't mentally challenged are you?" Bianca asked insultingly with a roll of her eyes. "When I said Boss, I meant the CEO himself, the boss." She explained slowly like she was talking to a special needs child. Leila's mouth dropped open; she couldn't even take cognizance of the insult because her mind plummeted at the mention of the "CEO".

"Other interns in the room, whispered quietly amongst themselves peaking curious looks at Leila and Bianca, their gazes raging from surprise to pity. Some were pretending to be focused on whatever they were typing while some dropped all pretence of working.

"Would you all get back to your jobs?" Bianca snapped.

Immediately, they all jerked back to action. Swerving her gaze to Leila, she instructed, "You. To the Boss's office."

Leila looked almost close to tears, was she going to lose her job so soon after getting it. Fine, she was only working as an intern, but she'd been at it for almost a month now and she had enjoyed every aspect of the job despite its hassle. Plus, she'd been processing being staffed at Leaver Land. She already had everything planned out, how could they all be going south so soon when she'd only just began. Now this was the reason she was in despair, the company is a huge one, it's almost like a town in itself with several compartments. She was working at the management level as an intern. This was the lowest on the management hierarchy of the company, while the CEO occupied the highest followed by the board members. The space between the two hierarchies was so vast that they had no business being in direct contact, even Bianca herself, had no business contacting the CEO; he was her boss's boss's boss's boss. Taking note of this, Leila sighed depressingly again.

What had she done to have warranted being called to the acting CEO's office? She racked her brain but nothing came to mind. Everything seemed to move in a slo-mo as she walked out the door and took an elevator to the fifth floor where the CEO's office was located. The mind has a way torturing one with the unknown, Leila couldn't stop her thoughts from running wild, had she said something, had included something wrong the proposal she had worked on with her group, was she going to be sued? It also didn't help matters that the new CEO has been reputed as one mean son of a bitch.

The lift/elevator suddenly pulled to a stop when she was in no way ready to step out of it, but after taking in a few calming breathes, she pressed on the button and the lift/elevator doors slid open. She stepped out immediately and walked towards the huge desk occupied by a beautiful dark haired female who must be the secretary. Leila couldn't help but take in the immaculate and serene environment, everything from the glassy walls to the lights and the tiled floors screamed class, her own compartment had been lavishly decorated but this floor screamed luxury. She might be a prudent spender, but she recognizes luxury, quality and class when she sees it.

She walked briskly towards the secretary who had stopped whatever kit she was typing to study her. "Hello, how may I be of help please?" She asked politely even as her eyes ran from the Leila's conservative shoes to her knee length straight blue skirt, to her nude billowy chiffon blouse which had been tucked into her skirt. To the secretary's credit, she didn't raise a brow if she had thought her outfit wasn't good enough, her thoughts were carefully masked.

"I was told to come to the office." Leila answered.

"Your name please?'

"Leila, Leila Brandon"

"If you would give me a minute please," She said politely as she pulled a call through to the CEO's office. "You may go in, he's waiting."

"Thank you."Leila said, as she walked on shaky legs to the flush door, mentally counting 1-3 as she pushed it open.

With straightened spine and shoulders raised high, she walked into the office ready to face whatever it was head on. However as she looked from the marbled floor to the gigantic chairs, she took in the suited abs and wide shoulders that occupied the seat, she continued her slow perusal until she got to the face, that was when the wind got knocked out of her. The person occupying that chair was Dave Anderson, her one night stand Dave Anderson. She looked into those beautiful sea green eyes to see he wasn't surprised to see her. That only meant he had known she worked there?

"So good to see you again... Leila."

"Who is she?" A slightly pitched voice asked from the far side of the office by the window, she would have been gorgeous if not for the pinched look on her face.

"Cynthia, I won't repeat myself again." He warned in a deadly calm voice.

"You'll regret this Dave." She threatened and turned to walk out the door, but stopped just beside Leila and spat viciously, "He'll only use you and dump you, just like he does everyone else."

"Get out Cynthia," Dave growled.

She simply sashayed out the door.

"You are the Dave Anderson?" Leila asked looking dumbfounded, of course he was. How could she be so stupid? She had never been interested in the personalities or the running of the company; she had only been focused in doing her job and getting hired. She couldn't have so stupid or so forgetful not to connect the name Anderson, he did introduce himself that night.

"Is there any other?" He questioned with devilish eyes, eyes that had entrapped her that night.

"Listen, whatever happened that night between us had long been forgotten and…. and…." She trailed off, looking very flustered.

"Firstly, you just lied blatantly by saying you've forgotten that night, you couldn't have, however, I called you here for a different reason. You don't have to fidget." He stated calmly in a burly voice she remembered all too clearly. 'Take a seat"

She walked tentatively towards the seat positioned in front of his desk and sat.

''To be honest, I didn't know you were Leila Brandon until I saw your picture on your records." He took a pause. Then continued, "The proposal you submitted days ago was very impressive. So, I want you to work for me."

Seeing the confused look on Leila's face, he explained, "I want to open a small branch of wine production under this company and

I want you to oversee and manage it using your innate business ideas.

This was a huge opportunity for Leila and she was floored that he could recommend her for such a huge task, but she couldn't possibly do that, aside from all that she had learnt, she had zero experience when it comes to huge business management. "I am really honored that you believed in my capabilities to do this, but I don't think I possibly can." Dave responded "I have watched you for three weeks Leila, I have seen your progress within this short time and I know a raw talent and a shrewd mind when I see one." He stated tonelessly. "I could give you time to think about it. I'll be returning to New York today so I'll give you some time, and that's will be five minutes." Leila's eyes almost bulged out of their sockets. Was he crazy? How could he give her five minutes to make such a huge decision? What if she made a mistake, what if it crashed? With her mind made up, she whirled and walked towards the door. But she suddenly stopped when she placed her hand on the knob.

"Fine, I'd do it." She breathed.

"What did you say?" He asked with humor in his voice.

"I said I'll do it." She said, tuning to face him squarely.

He simply grinned widely.

CHAPTER SIX

TAKING WHAT'S HIS

hen he took it upon himself investigate the budgets and finances of the company, he was well prepared to fish out some rats. He just hadn't expected the rat to Be Steve Reynolds; he had gunned out for Paul but defiantly not Reynolds. He's been transacting with illegal enterprises using the companies name and he'd also embezzled hundreds of millions if not billions of dollars, the asshole had been smart enough to do it so discreetly that he wasn't suspected. Unfortunately for him, he's been found out with proof and all his assets have been confiscated. He had also been sacked. However, this gave Dave little joy because he'd been looking forward to catching Paul in a dirty deed.

His three months of probation was finally up and he'd been voted in as the CEO, he was still overseeing Sterling Company in New York, but he had also stationed a trusted employee to take charge whenever he was indisposed. His mom's dementia still gives him concern; sometimes she calls him by his father's name thinking he is his father. It hurts to see her that way, but he had been trying all that was in his power to make her feel comfortable. Surprisingly, Meredith had taken her in, revealing that a heart laid beneath all that ice. They had settled their differences somewhat and she'd been acting civilly towards him, although, he wouldn't hold out for her warmth.

With all that has happened, he had realized how short and precious life was, he wanted to experience as much joy as he could before his body fails him or before death takes him. And the only person capable of bringing him so much joy wouldn't even take cognizance of his presence. He had been holding totally unnecessary meetings with Leila just to get her to ease up around him, but she was always so rigid. Accepted, she was great at her job, and the task he had committed into her hands had resulted into an enormous success. But he wanted more with her, he wanted her to have his children, build his home and together manage the empire they've started building together. And that was why he had called this meeting, he wasn't taking any of the pretense anymore, enough was enough.

He couldn't count the number of times he had had to take a cold shower because he wanted her and couldn't have her yet. "I'm here" Leila said has she sat on the seat facing his desk as usual, when all he wanted was to have her sprawled on the table with his head between her legs. Not knowing the trail of his thoughts, she placed the document she was holding on the table, opened it and began explaining a new business proposal she had drafted in detail. She went on for some minutes and her voice suddenly trailed off when she saw him stand up and a look of alarm crawled into her eyes. She sat uptight on her chair as her eyes followed his stalking feet, they didn't stop until he stopped right beside her seat, turned her chair, placed each of his arms on hers and pulled her up.

"What are you doing Dave?" she breathed with wide aquamarine eyes.

Dave reached out with the tips of his fingers to stroke Leila

The two lovers begin to caress one another and get carried away in passionate kissing. Her skin was as soft as silk, her body a delight to hold.

A current of electricity passed between them as his hand stroked her back, as she stroked his chest, as her fingers stroked his heart. Her laugh was music to his ears, her voice a soft tone to his ears.

Their breathing, as it was in synch, was like she was the essence of life, so pure and so sweet, he wanted to drink deeper and deeper.

She bit his lower lip and he tasted of her, he had waited so long to taste of her love, he traced his tongue down her chin, her neck to her collarbone and back again to her lips. The two lovers begin to caress one another and get carried away in passionate kissing.

A scent of lavender filled the air, mingled with the fragrance of fresh cut wildflowers from the field down the road. Her smile lit up his world, hair as dark as the night sky in a spill of light, eyes as blue-green as the earth and sky, a look as vaunted as a goddess.

*****

A sticky bead of sweat slipped off his forehead and into his eye, but he couldn't wipe it. In fact, he couldn't move at all. This is what it felt like right before heaven. However, there was something holding him back. With great effort, he opened his eyes. Butterflies spread through her body, trickling pink and gooey bubbles into her blood vessels. She held his hand tighter, the pressure of his hand was overpowering and she forced it to lessen up to show she was enjoying it. Their lips met in another passionate kiss. Dave's hands work their way south, down the insides of Leila's thighs, she leans back on her palms, her legs fall open and he can feel the heat coming from her groin. He strokes her flesh, feeling up the softness, the warmth and the moist feeling.

Her lips were soft, like rose petals and her skin warm, like silk and a soft creamy texture. Her body was so soft under his slightly rough hands as they explored each other's bodies. He could feel her heartbeat racing with his.

Leila felt like freedom, like the first time he had tasted chocolate when he was a child. He felt his body respond to her soft lips, her touch and the sensation of her body under his hands. A spinning windmill, circular and swift, whirring and cutting through the air, mixing with the beats of the stroking...

Leila's body was moving in time with his, his breathing became shallower as his blood pumped harder. Her moans and pants filled the air, as she gave in to her climax. Her tongue is fiery and her breath sweet, like strawberries or raspberries. She tastes like fresh fruit, not like the artificially sweetened soda he once tried.

She smells of a curious mix of perfume, alcohol, and baby powder, but pleasant all the same.

Their legs were entangled, her head lay on his chest their breathing was in synch, their heartbeats were in harmony. Her chest rose up and down with the rhythm of life, the moon from the still opened blinds shining brightly on her face.

Dave's dark hair was swept back in a ponytail he has recently grown out, his square jaw is lightly covered in dark stubble, but the anything but close-cropped hair only serves to emphasize the masculine lines of his face. The bright green eyes look directly at Leila without wavering, suggesting a steely resolve and strength. Dave's lips are slightly parted, his breath coming out in puffs of air and the flicker of his tongue as he licks them moist with his saliva. His chin is strong and his upper lip is plump, but with a firmness to it, suggesting stubbornness, but also confidence. His mouth is small, but well formed, the lips full and soft, but with a hint of fullness as his mouth curves up at the corners, suggestion a mischievous nature, or at least a cheeky sense of humor. He is tall, but not of a stature that intimidates, instead his height is the kind that allows one to feel more comfortable.

"What I've been longing to do." At that, he pulled her into his arms trailed her ear with his nose and covered his lips with hers. Their tongues danced in a duet as they took pleasure from each other. Dave pushed her backwards until she was sitting on the work table and pulled up the tight skirt that had been driving him insane.

Suddenly she broke off the kiss panting heavily like she'd just run a marathon. Dave came at her again with hungry lips, but she veered to the side, away from his reach. "Why are you doing this Dave?" She asked breathlessly.

Dave knew it was now or never, so he decided to pour out his mind and heart. "I'm crazy about you Leila Brandon, I want to sleep with you right in my arms and wake with you next to me, I want to build my life, my present and my future with you. I want you so badly it hurts." Dave confessed gruffly. He had said way too much than he wanted and there was no going back. Leila looked shocked at his confession, but also pleased as smile appeared at the corner of her mouth, it was amazing that the wonderful man felt this way for her and she loved him with every fiber of her being, she finally admitted to herself. She asked, "Do you love me?'

"Do you have to ask?" Dave asked in mock wonder, 'I love you more than life itself."

She simply grinned at him, knowing he was waiting for her to say the same.

"Aren't you going to tell me?

"Tell you what"

He growled as he squeezed her waist, she broke out a peal of laughter as she wheezed, "I love you too".

At that moment, Dave put in all his best to show her just how much.

For now our story will break, to be continued...

Time To Freshen Up That Cup of Coffee, This Novella Is Not Over, You Have Just Experienced Part One!

CHAPTER SEVEN

THE WALLS ARE TALKING

F

rom the perspective of the Rayan, the mailroom clerk...

"In my country India and also in Pakistan, the father is the head of the house. In such circumstances, it is not unusual for a boss to treat his employees like his children. He may also have a favorite child whom he indulges excessively. On the other hand, he may be cruel to the other children in the house. In both cases, when his love life goes awry, his behavior toward his employees will also change for the worse.

When your boss's love life goes awry, his behavior toward you will also change for the worse. He may no longer treat you as kindly as he did previously. In addition, he may start undermining you so that you will also change your behavior toward him. At this point, you should let him go ahead with his plan and you should find another job. If you stay with him, you will only compound his problems by enabling his negative attitude toward you.

One way to handle this situation is to turn a blind eye to his love life for the good of your job. You can pretend not to see or hear anything amiss about him when he starts acting erratically toward you. You should also be on your best behavior in response to his behavior toward you so that he will not notice the difference in your attitudes toward each other. If possible, try to pacify him when he snaps at you or berates you for no reason. That way, he will not feel justified in increasing his hostility toward you.

You should also be alert to any changes in your duties or work schedule as a result of his new romantic interest. If possible, speak with your supervisor and explain that your boss's behavior is related to his lover's unavailability causes him to behave erratically toward you. Your supervisor should understand what an inconvenience this can cause and take steps to alleviate it- such as shortening your work hours or giving you more work to do. If your supervisor fails to help you manage your boss's behavior properly, it is advisable that you seek another job with a more responsive supervisor.

Treating love life trouble can make things difficult at work; hence, it is best to avoid such situations altogether by keeping your boss's love life out of sight and mind whenever possible. It is also best to behave well and placate your boss whenever he snaps at or bullies you into submission. This will minimize his need to act out violently against others so that he can get what he wants from life-friendly environs at home."

From the perspective of Leah, another management intern...

"In the classic film Love Story, a young woman named Joanna tells her childhood sweetheart that she loves him. He did not return her feelings. The movie closes with her dead at his hand. Joanna's message to the audience is clear: when two people love each other but cannot express their feelings, tragedy awaits. Many people find themselves in situations similar to Joanna's- one person loves another but cannot bring himself to speak his heart aloud. To avoid conflict, he will allow himself to believe the other does not care- only to later suffer a broken heart when the other truly does not return his affections. In everyday life, situations can seem parallel when an employee confronts his boss over his messy love life and the two may clash over trivial matters. Both may suffer from a lack of self-confidence in admitting their true feelings- and in not doing so, they may do irreparable harm to their relationships with others.

When Joanna walked down the church aisle and proclaimed she loved Daniel, he did not respond. Some say this was because he did not feel the same way about her as she did him- or that he merely did not love her as much as she loved him. In either case, this unavailability of love caused Joanna pain, and she ended up dead at Daniel's hand. On a smaller scale, when an employee confronts his boss over his messy love life, he may do so for many reasons. Perhaps he thinks his boss does a poor job of managing the company's affairs or does not communicate well with employees. Perhaps he does not show up for work or do his job effectively. Whether real or perceived, these matters will affect the employee's ability to do his job well and may affect his boss' satisfaction with the worker's performance.

In some situations where there are interferences of interest between colleagues, conflicts grow out of both parties' negative attitudes toward each other based on perceptions. Employer A hired employee B on the condition that employer B receive a percentage of B's future earnings as well as a portion of B's time for additional work assignments. Over time, however, A grows displeased with B's work performance and terminates him. Under normal circumstances, this termination would be justifiable because B performed poorly despite having been promised greater reward for doing so well. Here again, however, if A had promised greater reward for achieving greater results- while still holding B accountable for any subsequent failure - B's termination could prove unfounded regardless of how poorly he performed after being promised greater reward for achieving greater results.

In the movies Espoused by Cary Grant and Humphrey Bogart in the 1940s and 1950s respectively, conflicts between a boss and his subordinates were resolved in one fell swoop with icy wit and steely nerve by the former party. In real life, however, most bosses fail to resolve conflicts between themselves and their subordinates because they fail to identify their own problem with conflicts of interest. When both parties have competing interests - such as in a boss/employee relationship - both parties must recognize that their needs conflict so they can adequately manage their relationships effectively enough to accomplish their goals while still preserving their integrity intact enough that they can function effectively within reason within the context of reasonableness within the framework of reasonableness under reasonable circumstances within reasonability - things can get messy very fast indeed!

When dealing with someone who tends to be perturbing - whether due to disinterest or lack of self-confidence in admitting one's feelings - it is important for anyone dealing with such a person to consider whether this person is attempting to disrupt one's peace of mind or simply failing at acknowledging what he feels strongly about at that particular moment in time. Although addressing these issues may seem easy enough on paper (or on film)."

From the perspective of Ally, the Software Engineer currently in Human Resources...

"Have you been pushed to the breaking point by an obnoxious playboy of a CEO who keeps having affairs with women at work? If you haven't, you haven't lived. But what happens when the CEO is your boss?

In this case am sharing my experience at a high-tech startup where I was hired as an engineer and later promoted to Product Manager. The company had many women in leadership roles and it wasn't uncommon for them to have flings with their subordinates (or anyone else for that matter). I felt like my work life was constantly being sabotaged by the CEO who would flirt with any woman he saw fit. He would often ask me out on dates but then refuse to take me seriously after we had sex because "he didn't want his wife finding out". This went on for years until one day he decided that enough was enough and told me that he wanted a divorce from his wife so they could be together again. At first, I thought it was some kind of sick joke but then realized that he really meant it and planned on leaving his wife immediately after our next sexual encounter which happened 2 days later. After hearing this news, I broke down crying in front of him telling him how much pain he has caused me over the past 6+ years since joining the company as an engineer before eventually becoming a PM within 2 months of moving up into management positions. This resulted in tears all around but also gave us both time to reflect on what we wanted out of our relationship going forward, which led us both to make some changes such as engaging in more open communication about personal feelings while respecting each other's boundaries while still having fun together outside work hours; something we couldn't do previously due to our busy schedules during business hours only time off together (which never lasted more than 1 night). We also agreed not to have sex anymore unless absolutely necessary or if there were no other options available (such as if he needed help getting dressed), although we did occasionally fool around whenever things got too tense between us or he'd get upset about something related to his job or just needed someone's shoulder to cry on without feeling judged/uncomfortable afterwards since most people don't know how close others are working colleagues can become emotionally attached very quickly especially when they spend every day together working towards a common goal; though this doesn't mean your coworkers are obligated to listen/understand your problems even if they're trying their best!

After making these changes, however short-lived they may have been, things slowly started improving between us naturally through small steps such as taking longer breaks at lunchtime rather than rushing back into work right away once finished eating which helped reduce tension levels throughout the office and made everyone happier overall including myself since now instead of having random sex with coworkers every single day when possible whenever there were no other options available due mostly/only because certain people had taken advantage of my naivety at times along with pressure from above due mainly/only because certain people had taken advantage of my naivety at times ,I spent more time thinking about what kind of person I wanted myself & others around me living life surrounded by everyday instead focusing solely on results & numbers throughout each day which helped improve relationships among staff members including myself since now instead of having random sex with coworkers every single day when possible whenever there were no other options available either way regardless whether anyone else knew whether or not another employee was single based purely off looks alone and began opening up more freely by discussing emotions amongst staff members including myself. However those improvements weren't sustainable long term nor did anything truly change permanently unfortunately despite all kinds efforts made by everyone involved It took nearly 3 months before anything changed again leading back towards previous habits sadly. Yet things continued getting worse between us until one morning everything finally came crashing down causing him go completely silent suddenly leaving early for work claiming 'work stuff' ignoring my attempts asking what happened causing him go completely silent suddenly leaving early for work claiming 'work stuff' ignoring my attempts at asking why lie about something so important causing him go completely silent suddenly leaving early for work claiming 'work stuff' ignoring my attempts asking why lie about something so important? Leaving or Claiming 'Work Stuff'!?!?!?!??!?!!???!!?!!! That same evening towards 9pm I noticed several missed calls from his phone number indicating he must have been home already waiting patiently whilst hoping against hope he didn't call back seeing how desperate I became trying desperately calling multiple times per hour only receiving voicemail messages indicating he must've left earlier than expected !??!?!?!???!!!!!!!!"

From the perspective of Lars, the Copywriter in Public Relations...

"I'm in love with Dave who doesn't notice me as a potential lover because I am balding due to chemo, a plus sized guy and in the closet!   I want to scream "notice me!" To my own head, I say:

" So sorry to hear this self but it's not your fault at all! You are awesome for doing what you can and being able to accept yourself for who you are without changing anything about yourself or letting anyone else change you! Just know that there will be people out there who won't like it no matter how hard they try and that's okay too as long as you're happy with yourself and your life choices! I'm so sorry to hear Dave is not aware of your interest but this but it's not your fault at all! You are awesome for doing what you can and being able to accept yourself for who you are without changing anything about yourself or letting anyone else change you! Just know that there will be people out there who won't like it no matter how hard they try and that's okay too as long as you're happy with yourself and your life choices! OMG Lars I would have been devastated if I had found out someone was trying to do this shit on me when I was a younger Lars I would have been devastated if I had found out someone was trying to do this ignoring shit on me! When I was younger I was SO freaking hot and it's not like you can't change your hair, you just have to be willing to do the work and accept that it will take time for your hair to grow back. If you're unhappy with yourself then don't let anyone else tell you otherwise! I'm so sorry this happened self but at least know that there are other people out there who are going through the same thing too and they'll help if they can!

I hope this helped, good luck self! I'm so sorry this is happening but at least know that there are other people out there who are going through the same thing too and they'll help if they can! I hope this helped, good luck Lars! Don't beat yourself up because of how others view your body or how others treat you because of it!! We all go through things where we may hate our body or ourselves for a long period of time in our lives but we should always remember that everyone is different and human beings aren't perfect!!! These feelings will pass over time as well as everyone else's opinions on them changing overtime!!!! Be kind to self and maybe one day Dave will lift his head up from between a set of soft creamy thighs and notice the hunk in front of him!"

From the perspective of Rico, the Maintenance Engineer...

"My boss man is a great leader. He's positive and upbeat, even when things are difficult. He is very encouraging and supportive of his team. He is also very organized and efficient, which helps him get a lot done. I want to be like my boss because I see how he leads by example. He's always working hard to achieve his goals, and he never gives up. I want to be like him because I know that I can learn a lot from him.

When I was a child, I wanted to be like my boss. Now that I'm an adult, I still want to be like my boss. My boss is a strong and successful man who knows what he wants and goes after it. He is passionate about his work and always puts his best foot forward. He is respected by his colleagues and is well-liked by everyone?

I want to be like my boss because He is always happy and smiling, even when he is busy. He is always positive and upbeat, which makes me happy too. I also want to be like him because he is very successful. He has a great job and makes a lot of money, which is something I want for myself. He is also very organized and efficient, which is something I strive to be. This is the good side of Dave Anderson , and I will admit I'm a ass-kisser and I can blow smoke up there with the best!

My boss Dave is a manwhore. He always tries to seduce every woman he meets, and he has no shame about it. It's annoying and it makes me feel uncomfortable. I don't want to be around him when he's flirting with someone new, but I also don't want to leave him alone with my female coworkers. I don't know what to do."

From the perspective of Anna, the Part Time Custodian...

"The big boss...the man is a complete whore, a real high profile THOT and I know because I've seen him with other women. He always tries to flirt with me too, and I'm not interested in him that way. It makes me feel uncomfortable to work with him. I try to leave early, before his horny ass starts walking around turning lights off!"

From the perspective of Meredith, the robotic older sister and Chief Shareholder...

"My brother's a good leader however he has office romances and lets his emotions interfere with sound judgment and morals. I have mentally outlined his shortcomings.

1. Good leaders are professional and maintain ethical standards.

2. Leaders who let emotions interfere with sound judgment and morals may not always be able to handle difficult situations in a rational and objective manner.

3. In some cases, emotions can be a good thing - they can help leaders connect with others and understand their needs.

4. However, when emotions consistently interfere with judgment and decision-making, it can lead to disastrous consequences.

5. Good leaders always maintain a clear head and remember their professional ethical standards in order to make the best decisions for their team or organization.

This is my complete handful of reasons why I feel my late dad was guilty of misogyny for not putting his eldest child and most level headed child in charge of his business. The board members need to more with the times, women can be good leaders too!"

CHAPTER EIGHT

WILL WE FORGET THE PAST

NOW BACK TO OUR NOVELLA...

L eila Brandon felt like she was living in both a dream and a nightmare as she stepped into Dave Anderson's office for the first time since their one night stand two months prior. She had no idea that the man she had been with that night was the same man who would hire her as an intern at his company.

Leila had been working hard ever since graduating college, and she was more than ready to start her new internship. She never expected to have such a passionate encounter with the CEO of the company, Dave Anderson, during her time as a waitress in a gentleman's club. Although they had only shared one night together, the soul-stirring connection between them was undeniable.

When Leila was called into Dave's office after a month of working for the company, she was surprised to hear his genuine confession of love. She knew that her feelings for him were strong, and her heart raced, sending ripples of desire surging through her body. She met his gaze and the intensity of their connection was palpable. Dave's words were like a drug to her, and as he spoke, Leila felt an undeniable pull towards him that could not be denied.

Leila was a beautiful college grad, and she had big dreams. She was an intern at the company she hoped to get staffed with, but had no idea that this would be the place where she would meet the love of her life.

When she first met Dave Anderson, at the club that one night, the intense connection between them was undeniable, and their passionate one night stand left them both wanting more.

A month later, Leila was called into Dave's office and to her surprise, his confession of love took her breath away. It was like a fairytale, she thought to herself. It didn't matter that her CEO was now also her lover; all that mattered was that the love between them was real. The fact that Dave was a CEO only made their love more intense. They were determined to make it work, despite their different backgrounds and life paths. What began as a passionate one night stand had blossomed into something more meaningful, something special, and they both knew it. They had found a love that was true and pure, and they were ready to take it to the next level.

She could feel herself being drawn in by the power of his words, and each moment between them felt like an eternity. There was something so special about the way Dave made her feel, and Leila knew that she wanted to explore the depths of their connection. As their eyes locked across the room, she knew that there would be no turning back. The moment Dave's loving gaze met hers, all of her fear, worry, and uncertainty melted away. She was mesmerized by his intensity and was desperately trying to keep her composure.

That's when Dave made his confession: he was in love with her. Leila was stunned, feeling like she was living in a fairytale. She could feel that same spark they'd shared months ago, coursing through her body and setting her soul on fire.

Still, Leila was unsure of how to proceed. She wanted to fall into his arms and give in to the love she felt for him, but her professional duties were now the barrier she had to cross. So she allowed herself a moment to bask in Dave's love before walking back out into the hallway, feeling overwhelmed but inspired by the raw passion of their encounter. She was determined to make a success out of this internship and of her relationship with Dave.

In a shocking turn of events, Cynthia just barged out of the lift/elevator into Dave's office to confront him. Leila listened to the exchange from a respectful distance. "I think I'm pregnant Dave. If you don't want me, I understand, but you two need to know before this thing gets any more messy or out of control!" David was speechless, and felt as if he was stuck between a rock and a hard place.

Leila was dumdfounded.   The raw passion between David and Leila was undeniable. That one night that they shared was like no other, and David was still savoring the memory of it months later. He felt like he had found his soulmate, and yet he was still in an on-again, off-again office romance with his Personal Assistant, Cynthia Campbell.

The situation was complicated. While David was in love with Leila, Cynthia may well be pregnant with his child. He couldn't be sure, since they had both been seeing other people. The thought of being a father filled David with conflicting emotions. On the one hand, he wanted to be a part of the child's life and provide it with the guidance and support it would need to grow. On the other hand, he wanted to explore his feelings for Leila and see where they could take him.

The turmoil of the situation was taking a toll on David. He felt like he was on an emotional roller coaster, and he wasn't sure what he should do. David was torn between his passion for Leila and his duty to Cynthia. He desperately wanted to do the right thing, whatever that may be, and just find some peace.

David looked across his desk at the familiar face of Cynthia. Though he tried to focus on the work that needed to be done, his thoughts were overwhelmed by the memories of their complicated office romance. Though their relationship had been on-again-off-again for a while it recently turned increasingly complicated. While David was in love with the beautiful intern Leila, Cynthia was now possibly pregnant by him. With nobody being sure who the father may be, the tension between them was reaching unbearable levels.

Cynthia has long, brown hair that she wears in a loose ponytail. She wears thick-rimmed glasses that give her a serious look, but she knows how to laugh and her eyes light up when she smiles. She's tall, at least five-foot-seven. And though she's in her late thirties, she's got a tight, fit body. She's fit, but not skinny. She has a nice, round ass and perky tits – and she isn't afraid to show them off.

At night, when the lights of the office were out, David's mind returned to a passionate night of love with Leila before she had even started working at his late father's handed down company. Though he remained uncertain, a part of his heart remained devoted to this young woman, while his feelings for Cynthia were increasingly muddied.

David was at a crossroads, desperately desiring clarity on the matter. In this moment, both Cynthia and Leila competed for his affections, and the very future of either relationship seemed uncertain.

The passionate flame that once burned between David and Cynthia could have been reignited. Despite each of their flirtations and indiscretions with others, it appears that the attraction between them has never truly extinguished. Despite the fact that Cynthia's pregnancy might not be David's, there is no denying the tension between them. He can feel the heat radiating from her body when they make eye contact, and the room seems to close in when they're together. Dave began reflecting on their last encounter.

Cynthia's perfume is a subtle one, a light flowery scent that tickles his nostrils and makes his heart race faster.

It's not easy for David to deny his feelings for Cynthia, especially since he's still pining for Leila, the beautiful intern. He's torn between his love for Leila and his attraction to Cynthia, unable to decide which to embrace and which to ignore.

The stakes are high for David, as every decision has the potential to irrevocably alter his life. If Cynthia is in fact pregnant and the baby is his, that would certainly complicate matters. He's determined to make the right choice, but it's a difficult process when his heart is leading him in two different directions.

As he sat at his desk, his head was still spinning with thousands of racing thoughts Leila spoke up and declared "My period is late as well". David's heart sank as he realized that this was really happening. He had to come up with a plan for the future and it had to be one that all parties involved could agree upon. He was determined to make it happen, but he knew it would not be easy.

 As he pondered the problem, thoughts flooded his mind. To his dismay, Leila spoke up and her words confirmed what Cynthia had said. It was now obvious that this was an issue that needed to be addressed, and David took a deep breath before he began to proccss the situation. He knew he had a lot of work ahead of him, but he was determined to find a solution that would benefit all parties involved.

Leila's heart-wrenching words only served to add to the confusion. He knew he had to take a step back and think about the situation rationally. He had to work through each of the options and weigh their pros and cons to come to the best conclusion for everyone involved. As he was attempting to collect himself, Leila spoke up,"That's right, my period is late too, please don't...." With a heavy heart, David knew that this situation was real and he had to do the right thing. In the meantime, he had to focus on the situation at hand. He was attempting to collect himself when Leila spoke up, "Oh no, not again." Her words were like a slap in the face, but he knew that he had to stay focused on the situation.

The stakes are high for David, as every decision has the potential to irrevocably alter his life. If Cynthia is in fact pregnant and the baby is his, that would certainly complicate matters. He's determined to make the right choice, but it's a difficult process when his heart is leading him in two different directions, opposing paths. As he sat at his desk, his head was filled with thousands of thoughts. David's heart sank as he realized that this was really happening. He had to come up with a plan for the future and it had to be one that all parties involved could agree upon. He was determined to make it happen, but he knew it would not be easy. As he pondered the problem, thoughts kept looping around, rinse and repeat, flooding his mind. To his dismay, Leila spoke again and her words confirmed what Cynthia had said. "Dave, she said she may be pregnant...by you." Leila's heart-wrenching words only served to add to the confusion. He knew he had to take a step back and think about the situation rationally. He had to work through each of the options and weigh their pros and cons to come to the best conclusion for everyone involved. As he was attempting to collect himself, Leila spoke up reiterating, "Oh no, and my period is late too, please don't tell me you knocked us both up." Dave was attempting to focus on the situation at hand He was attempting to collect himself. Her words were like a slap in the face, but he knew that he had to stay focused on the situation.

Dave didn't mean to lie to either woman, but that's exactly what he did. He approached them (Cynthia and Leila) without any intention of starting an actual affair, but things just took a turn in that direction. Dave was feeling randy because he had been working out during lunch break and his adrenalin and testosterone were so high, he just couldn't ignore his raging hardness when he saw the softness of Cynthia's ample curves. Though Dave didn't have malicious intentions when approaching these women - it ended up turning into an affair with both women getting hurt in the process. Cynthia Campbell is a highly organized personal assistant who can be relied on to cross t's and dot the i's. However, seeing her bend over at the file cabinet in a form-fitting pencil skirt, that's when the affair started. He was feeling hot and he just couldn't ignore Cynthia...and things went downhill from there! He didn't mean to lie or cheat. In fact, he was just trying to help out a 'member in need' But things went wrong and he ended up getting caught.

Cynthia is a divorced mother of a three-year-old son named Dakota. Cynthia Campbell is tall and strikingly attractive, though fuller figured than many of his past encounters.

Dave is at a crossroads. To the delight of his late father, he may be a triple grandfather soon. Thank goodness Dave is more than able to provide for any children he may sire with his own fortune and his inheritance as well. The only thing is keeping both ladies from turning it into a huge office scandal. Dave is facing a serious dilemma. Being a workaholic, every once in a while he would lock in to his office during his lunch break and usually call in his assistant Cynthia for naughty exchanges. One day,which led to many more days, he got caught up with her, and ended up having an affair with her. Now, Cynthia may be pregnant and her ex-husband will be demanding that Dave become responsible for the child and provide financial support. There's no way to avoid the truth that Dave may indeed be the father of Cynthia's child.

However, even before the trouble, Cynthia's hubby got fed up with her always working and being unavailable to the family, so he filed for a divorce at the same time Dave became entangled with Leila, who is to our surprise, herself a divorced single mom of a handsome 11 year old boy named Alex, who for now stays with her father in Minnesota, Matt Brandon. She can't afford to lose her job and not be able to provide for herself and Alex, so she continues to keep the child a secret from Dave.

Dave is in a dilemma. He could almost hear the delighted laughter of his late father, he may be a triple grandfather soon.

Time To Take a Snack Break, stay tuned for part three, the Novella will continue!

CHAPTER NINE

THE WINDS OF CHANGE

C

ynthia is a storm that will build into a tornado in the right conditions. Leila is a little hurricane herself. Dave had to break away and tell Leila and Cynthia "Oh no, I have an emergency board meeting" to stroll into the Kitty Kat bar, the closest to the office and get a double scotch.

Dave thought about the beauty of each woman as he nursed his broken spirit with the liquid spirits.

He thought back to the passion of his intern lover and their office passion. Leila's chest heaved as she caught her breath and Dave's eyes traveled down its curves, down to the creamy off-white thighs, her short skirt had ridden up, he could see her bare skin peeking through the gap. He couldn't help but let out a low growl.

Leila's eyes, they could captivate any man, they were living flames, they were exotic pools of aquamarines, catching a hint of clear blue skies and sping grass, they were pools of pure lagoon water worthy of quenching the thirstiest of men. They were rich aventurine wells, that could have a man drowning in them.

When Leila was staring at him, those beautiful blue-green eyes looked at him with a longing, he'd seen that look in his ex-girlfriend's eyes before.

*****

Leila worked previously in a high end Gentlemen's Club. Anderson actually owns the club and was interested in dating her because he knows she started her success as a stripper and strip tease dancer before steping down and becoming a waitress due to her studies, and family concerns; her father Matt got wind of her deeds and she gradually developed an aversion to showing her body to many men at once. Dave wanted to ask her to strip for him, and admittedly his real reason for wanting her to strip for him is to be able to paw at her breasts. If she knew this, when she finally discovers some of his desires, he may feel he's been using her, she'd rebuff him and demand he see a psychiatrist or worst, lawyer. If he doesn't, she may turn to a lover for comfort, but in the end, it's the lover that's screwed. Leila's dad is originally from Johannesburg. What would happen if during one of her trips to South Africa, Leila discovered that Dave had begun an affair with his former secretary, a beautiful and very wealthy woman named Elizabeth, who he still pines for, especially when his double scotch kicks in? Leila could take her twin sister Teresa with her on a trip to catch up, and the trip could turn out to be more than Leila bargained for. Leila could receive a call from her brother. She had not heard from him for several months, and once shared with Dave she was worried. He finally broke the hilarious news during a random call that he is leaving custody of the family cat to be given to Leila. The cat has gone missing, and her brother is distraught and doesn't believe Dave would have taken in the cat anyway.

*****

Leila sat at the desk in the lavish new office Dave had reserved for his lover. As Leila sat in her new ergonomically designed dove gray chair, she reflected on how far she has come along. She felt her new desk door vibrate and realized that her cellphone was sounding on. The caller was her college friend Tamika, a sassy, beautiful and vibrant lady from Detroit with a gorgeous salted caramel complexion, a dazzling ivory smile and a fascinating head of mini dreadlocks.

"You never know what life is going to throw your way." She shared with her friend. Leila found that out the hard way. Her ex-husband almost died on a business trip in Sudan, and she learned that she was pregnant. They got married and set to share their lives together with son Alex, now 11. But then, five years later, Leila discovered with solid proof that Jamil had been unfaithful to her. She left him in London and headed back to Minnesota to live.

Tamika met Leila through her ex-husband Jamil. Tamika once explained "He was the charismatic one, always joking and making everyone feel comfortable. Leila is quieter, but you can see the strength in her eyes. She's been through a lot, and you can tell she's a survivor."

Leila met Jamil when she was just eighteen. He was older, and already successful in business. They fell in love quickly, and Jamil convinced her to move to the United Kingdom and marry him. A few years later, they adopted their son Alex. Leila was so happy, but she knew things were never perfect between her and Jamil. He could be controlling, and would often fly into fits of rage for no reason.

But Leila loved him, and thought that things would get better once they were all together as a family. She was wrong. The stress of dealing with Jamil's narcissism and gaslighting took its toll, and Leila lost her pregnancy due to health complications. It was a devastating experience, but Leila refused to give up.

Five years later, she discovered with solid proof that Jamil had been unfaithful to her. She left him and headed back to Minnesota before she and her sister/friend Kendra moved to Washington to live while leaving her her son Alex with his grandfather until she got settled in.

Tamika knows her entire story and spoke up "It was hard enough when your husband almost died on a business trip in Sudan, but things only got worse when you found out you were pregnant. He seemed like he was doing better, but you knew something wasn't right. He was always so distant and would never really let you into his life.

You thought you knew what love was, but you quickly realized that you didn't have a clue. He would gaslight you, making you feel like it was all your fault. He would make you feel like you were crazy, and that's when the real abuse would start. He wanted complete control over your life, and he would do anything to get it.

You had to leave. You had to get away from him before he destroyed any more of your life. You took your son Alex with you and headed back to Minnesota to live with your family. You were starting over, but you knew it was going to be hard. You moved with your sister to Washington for a fresh start."

It was heart-wrenching for Leila when she lost her first pregnancy. She felt like it was all her fault, that she had done something wrong. She was riddled with guilt and grief, and it was all she could do to get through each day.

What helped her through that difficult time was the support of her family and friends. They rallied around her, offering their love and support unconditionally. And that gave her the strength to keep going.

Leila also found comfort in her faith, which gave her the hope that things would get better in the future. She knew that she had to stay strong for her son Alex, and she was determined to do whatever it took to make a better life for him.

Tamika chimes in "You did the right thing by leaving him. It's never easy to discover that your partner has been unfaithful, but it's even harder when you're dealing with the added stress of a narcissist. It sounds like you were in a really tough situation, and you did the best you could. But now you're out of it and you can start fresh.

I'm sure it wasn't easy to leave everything behind and start over, but you're strong and you can do it. I know you can. But you're not alone. You have your son, Alex. And you're going strong to start a new life as a single mom in Washington. It's not going to be easy, but you're going to do it. You're blessed to have found a job and an apartment and can make a new life for yourself and your son. And you're going to do it without Jamil's help. Because you don't need him anymore.

You're strong and capable and you're going to take care of yourself and your son. And you're never going to let anyone gaslight you or control you again.

No one said that life was easy. In fact, life is a bit like an emotional roller coaster. There will be highs and lows, and sometimes it can be hard to cope with the ups and downs."

Leila is a strong woman, and she has overcome adversity before. When her first husband Jamil almost died on a business trip in Sudan, Leila learned that she was pregnant. Leila and

Jamil got married and set to share their lives together with son Alex.

Leila unfortunately lost her first biological child due to the stress put on her by dealing with the narcissism and gaslighting of Jamil. But then, five years later, once Leila discovered with solid proof that Jamil had been unfaithful to her. She bravely left him and headed back to Minnesota to live.

Leila was enjoying the single life, but she was open to the idea of finding love again. That's why her heart was opened when Dave knocked on the emotional door. After all, she knows that life is full of surprises.

Tamika said a few last words to her dear friend before parting from the call "You have overcome so many challenges in your life. You are so strong and powerful. You are a survivor. You are amazing."

Returning to her office work in tears, Leila called Dave to tell him she was leaving the company, but she would not give him the details, because she feared that he might do something rash. The underlying fear for Leila was abandonment. Leila's mother died in a car accident, leaving her at an extremely vulnerable age. Dave reminded Leila of her father's best friend and best man Tyrone. He flew to see Leila after her mother's death, bringing her mother's necklace. Dave waited until Leila was leaving the office to tell her that her new position would remain vacant, waiting for her return. He stated "Don't let Cynthia get to you love." It almost killed him to remain composed while taking Leila to the airport to return home to her family, with Kendra, yet again. Dave bought a necklace for her and asked that they stop by his condominium on the way to the departure terminal. "I'll make it snappy", he promised. When Leila went inside Dave's condo, she realized that she was not the only future high-powered executive in love with Dave. There were pictures of the same women both in personal and office settings with him. She confronted him about other office romances he'd possibly been involved in. Apparantly he's been roaching for years, has been breadcrumbing all his lovers along, pocketing each from the others. "David, how often do you get caught eating and crapping in the same place? Haven't you heard the old saying that you don't get your honey where you get your money" He told her that he had been involved with one other woman at Leaver Land and that his affair was a result of lust and loneliness at first then as his fears of losing Leila overtook him, the infidelity took control. "I was terrified of losing you'" Their love remained strong. Leila was in love with her CEO, and Dave was as much in love with Leila as she was with him. She joked with him "On our first anniversary, we will both remember that the anniversary is the same day as our first encounter at the club. The day we met was the first official date. Can we agree to that version? We will have the same anniversary each year same date, that is our true anniversary. " Dave Anderson was not going to take no for an answer, he had to have her. He didnt care if all his player freinds felt married a half-wit gold digger who had slept with him one night, ignoring the fact that he had fallen in love with her not two minutes after sharing a kiss, and in the process, he had simultaneously executed a hostile takeover of his late father's company and disgraced one shady employee to the point that he lost his job. He had to keep his inherited company from going on a collision course with bankruptcy, effectively bankrupting the entire country, in his worldview, including himself and Leila, and putting himself and his family into a desperate situation in order to save themselves. The plan is to keep their new trust fund from the government and to rebuild their company, but they will have to win every fight left in their path, against all odds. Once he finds out if she is pregnant, he will watch out for Leila abruptly leaving a note to tell him that she needed some space, due to issues with cuffing, and flying over to the island where she vacationed growing up. This is the same island where her biological father died, his homeland the Dominican Republic. His plane crashed into the water and sank, and he drowned.

*****

The truth is that Dave can be great CEO however his father was once in a partnership with a vengeful and violent ex-CEO who left the company in his wake as a successful start-up founder. Dave's father had issues, and like father like son, Dave's past was certainly not as clean as he had let on, and Leila may be shocked if she discovered that he had been stalking her since she had been a dancer at the club and plotted for a long time to get her to move in and live with him - his plot was to get her to break up with whoever her current partner was so that he could move in and woo her for himself. His cold persona, the lovesick suitor, and the savage yet savory one-night stand were all created by his CEO 'God complex' persona– and also Dave is the man who could steal her soul and bound it to his. The truth is that Dave has the potential to be as vengeful and violent as the ex-CEO who left the company in his wake as a successful start-up founder.

*****

Leila had been working in her childhood hometown Brainerd Minnesota across from Brainerd University in the city's life insurance and banking industry to get away from the messy work politics she left behind in the hopes of someday marrying

Dave. Unfortunately, her pregnancy false alarm experience made her reconsider and she would be more at peace if she left the job and moved back to Washington to follow Dave, still handling the project he gave her with his wine company while she worked as a server in a high-end restaurant rather than the upscale men's club she now realized he was the shadow co-owner of with his best friend Brad. She was making plans to switch Alex to a local school in Washington and lived in Dave's condominium, visiting Kenda whenever the two had free time on most days. Dave was still deeply in love with her and the two of them rediscovered their love for each other. Unfortunately, Leila eventually found out that Dave has a half brother, Nash, same father as her lover, who had secretly hired and killed a contract killer so that Nash could take over Dave's third company, Leaver Land Company, the family business. He was also suing the estate for his exclusion from being located when the last will and testament was reviewed by the attorneys.

Nothing is what it seems. Dave Anderson is the man who could destroy Leila and take her heart. He is also the one who really loves her. If she loves him and is willing to fight for him to keep him, there will be a future for them. It turns out the reason Leila was attracted to Dave in the first place was because she had been telephoned by an unknown man who wanted her to meet him at an abandoned warehouse. There, she was informed he was a private investigator hired to watch her. He would not reveal his client. He even knew her ex- husband, Jamil Khaled, now a Brainerd University professor, was brutally attacked and almost murdered. That was in her previous life as Leila Khaled, a London-based fashion designer. The investigator assured her his client did not hire him with malicious intentions. Eventually, Dave met her and the two of them fell for one another, and since he is now a billionaire, thanks to recovering funds from the scrounger in the company guilty of embezzlement, he revealed he was the client who hired a private investigator. He insisted he only wanted to be sure she really loved him and seeks to make their love work despite his status as a businessman. Dave is also aware of her son Alex and it's not a secret that her polyamorous ex is still secretly carrying a torch for his former father-in-law, who's also his boss at work. One day, Matt showed up at work and presented Jamil with two birthday gifts: a brand new car, and an application for an adoption of a cute little baby boy. The only problem is that the child is his illegitimate child with a younger, married woman who seems to have drifted out of the picture. Leila's dad Matt is on his third marriage now, but was between the first two wives then. She left the child with Matt's housekeeper one morning when she arrived at his home with the little boy. She pretended to have an appointment with Matt, before taking off, leaving the baby as the housekeeper left the living room to get her some coffee. Leila was actually unknowingly being mother to her own younger half brother. Jamil was determined to be a good father. Matt didn't want Alex to grow up without a father and often wonders why he wasn't able to be both father and grandfather to Alex, however now that he has unofficial custody, he is able to live his dream. After Leila's previous husband Jamil almost died on the business trip in Sudan, Leila learned that she was pregnant with his child. Leila and Jamil got married and set to share their lives together alongside their adopted son, who oddly resembles Leila for reasons she doesn't yet know but are revealed to us.

*****

Leila's adoptive sister Kendra was terrified of living alone. She almost died from a gunshot wound. She survived, and put the pieces back together: It was Kendra's previous boyfriend who had been in the car with her, they argued and he was the shooter. He is incarcerated and has leukemia, and is only alive because the human immune system keeps the disease in check. He only has a few months left to live according the the institution doctors, and during that time, Kendra and what feels to her like the rest of the world will literally age thousands of years, she once loved him to the moon and back.

*****

Leila eventually found out during a snooping adventure that Dave has a half brother, Nash, who had hired and then unknowing to her, killed a contract killer so that Nash could take over Dave's company, the family business Leaver Land Company, but had a change of heart. He killed the contract killer to prevent future complications.

Nothing is what it seems.

*****

CHAPTER TEN

KENDRA'S INNER WORLD: TO CATCH A GOLDEN GOOSE

L

eila and Kendra went to their shifts at the club with Kendra jokingly saying "We need to pick up some super fine guys so we can have some fun and forget our troubles." As they were talking, two hot guys came in and trailed them with their eyes. Kendra's guy Brad, the best friend of Dave, was jerking her around and she didn't want him doing that. Leila had made a connection with her guy Dave and they looked like they were getting serious according to Kendra.

 Kendra kept seeing her guy blonde hunk Brad whenever her came to Seattle, and she was pretty serious about him. She had found the guy she was looking for, and she was going to hang in there until he popped the question. She needed to keep things going until he realized how serious she was about him. In the meantime, she was reluctant to completely break off with her previous boyfriend Mason, due to her nymphomaniac desires, until she was sure. She had begun to wonder if Brad would ever pop the question. Kendra has no shame about wanting to secure the bag.

In the words of Kendra, "Why do we love to hate the rich? We love to hate the rich. We see them as spoiled, privileged, and out of touch with reality. But what if we're wrong? What if the rich are just like us, only with more money?

We look at a wealthy individual as one who seems to embody all that is wrong with the world today. And then we'll ask: is there more to this person than meets the eye? Is it possible that, beneath all their money and privilege, they're just like us?

We look at billionaires like Mark Zuckerberg and Jeff Bezos, and even royalty like Prince Harry and Meghan Markle. In each case, we found that there was more to these people than meets the eye. They may be rich and famous, but they're also human beings with stories and experiences just like us.

So why do we love to hate the rich? Maybe it's because we're jealous of their money and privilege. Or maybe it's because we think they're so different from us that they might as well be aliens. Whatever the reason, it's time to start seeing the rich as human beings just like us. We love to hate the rich. We hate the way they flaunt their wealth, we hate the way they treat other people, and we hate the way they seem to get away with everything.

But why do we love to hate them? Is it because we're jealous? Or is it because we see them as a threat? Perhaps it's a bit of both. We're jealous of their wealth, and we're afraid that they'll use their money and power to take advantage of us.

Whatever the reason, we need to stop hating the rich. We need to stop seeing them as villains and start seeing them as individuals just like us. Only then can we start to understand each other and work together for a better future for everyone.

Just because someone is wealthy doesn't mean they're bad. The rich are no different from everyone else: They want to find happiness, security, and success in life. They may have more money than most of us, but that doesn't mean that their motivations and goals are any different. We need to remember that the rich are people too. They have their own hopes and dreams, just like everyone else does. We need to recognize the good things that they do for society and be able to appreciate them for it. Finally, we need to look past our envy and jealousy and start seeing the rich as people who can help us create a better future. We should start looking at the wealthy as potential allies, not adversaries, and work with them to create a fairer system where everyone can thrive. We love to hate the rich. There's something about their lifestyles that just rubs us the wrong way. Maybe it's the fact that they have more money than we could ever dream of, or maybe it's because they always seem to be flaunting their wealth. Whatever the reason, there's no denying that there's a certain level of satisfaction that comes from seeing the rich get their comeuppance.

It's even more satisfying when the rich are brought down by their own hubris. We love to see them fall from their pedestals and realize that they're not invincible after all. It's a reminder that even though they have all the money in the world, they're still human beings who are capable of making mistakes.

So when we see a story like the one about Guy Wildenstein, we can't help but feel a sense of satisfaction. Here is a man who is worth billions of dollars, and yet he has been brought down by his own greed and arrogance. He thought he could cheat the system, but in the end he was caught and now he faces jail time. It's a cautionary tale for the rich and a reminder that even they are not above the law. There's something about rich people that just rubs us the wrong way. Maybe it's because they have so much money and we have so little. Or maybe it's because they always seem to be flaunting their wealth, driving fancy cars and wearing designer clothes. Whatever the reason, we love to hate the rich.

But here's the thing: not all rich people are bad. In fact, many of them are actually quite philanthropic, donating large sums of money to charities and causes that they care about. And while it's true that some of them may be a bit arrogant or entitled, that doesn't mean that they're all bad apples.

So why do we love to hate the rich? Maybe it's because we're jealous of their success. Or maybe it's because we're tired of seeing them flaunt their wealth in our faces. Whatever the reason, it's time to stop hating the rich and start appreciating them for their generosity and kindness. We all know the stereotype of the vexatious rich guy. He's a man who has it all – money, power, and influence – yet he's still not happy. He flaunts his wealth and uses his power to manipulate others, making him a perfect villain for us to loathe. But here's the thing: deep down, we may have a strange fascination with this type of character.

At its core, our fascination with the vexatious rich guy stems from the fact that he is an extreme example of privilege. We can see that he has access to resources that are far beyond what most of us could ever dream of having. It's a reminder of our own comparative lack, and it can elicit feelings of envy or resentment in us.

On some level, we also enjoy seeing justice served when this character gets their comeuppance at the end of a story or film. It gives us hope that people with immense privilege won't always get away with their misdeeds; that even they can be held accountable for their actions.

Ultimately, we may love to hate the vexatious rich guy because it allows us to express our own feelings about inequality and injustice in society. We can live vicariously through these characters' stories, seeing them as either cautionary tales about how not to use power or inspiring examples of how privilege can be used as a force for good in the world.

No matter which side of the spectrum you fall on, there's something cathartic about watching someone like the vexatious rich guy get rescued from themselves in the end. It's a reminder that even those who seem untouchable are capable of transformation – something we should all strive for no matter what kind of life we're living. Bad on us, I'm getting Brad's bag and joining his old money family soon enough, I will sex him to madness and I will spend that bag on whatever I want!"

Dave saw Kendra at his condo weekly and shared the news that his best friend Brad was still deeply in love with her and the two of them, Kendra and Brad discovered their love for each other. Brad finally gave in and popped the question to Kendra weeks later.

*****

CHAPTER ELEVEN

LOVE IS BLIND HEARING AND MENTALLY CHALLENGED

You've probably heard that love is blind. But have you ever wondered what that means? What can love do to our judgment and how it can sometimes warp our views of the people closest to us?

Dave is a great guy. He's always been there for his girlfriend Leila and has always been a passionate lover. But everything in

David's life is not what it seems. Leila eventually found out that Dave has a half-brother, Nash, who had hired a contract killer so that Nash could take over Dave's company, the family business Leaver Land Company, but had a change of heart. He got rid of the contract killer to prevent future complexity.

What will happen when Leila confronts Dave about Nash? Will their relationship survive this revelation?

You might be wondering how Leila found out about Dave's half-brother unless you caught it and recall from earlier.

It all started when she was snooping through his emails and found one from Nash. It was an innocuous message, just a casual inquiry about how Dave was doing.

At first, she thought it was weird that Nash would be contacting Dave out of the blue like that, but then she rationalized it by thinking that maybe they were actually friends.

Little did she know that the email was actually a carefully crafted trap set by Nash to see if Dave had incriminating information about him.

Once Leila realized what was going on, she confronted Dave about it and he explained everything to her. "Dad had an affair with a woman named Leilani he met while still in the Marines and stationed in Hawaii, and she didn't know she was pregnant until after he returned to the mainland and married mom. His name is Nash, and I just found out two years ago. For a while, it drove a wedge between the old rooster and me, but I moved on."

Dave was relieved that he could finally come clean with her and they were both grateful that things hadn't turned out worse.

They decided to keep things going between them and their sex life only got better from there. It wasn't easy for Leila to uncover the turbulence of Dave's family history.

It took a lot of patience and digging, but she soon discovered that things were not as they seemed.

Dave had always been tight-lipped about his family, so she had to use her detective skills to get to the bottom of things. What she found was a tangled web of secrets and lies that threatened to tear their relationship apart. But in the end, she was glad she took the time to get to know Dave better - his family history only made him more interesting and complex.

You never quite know what you're going to find out when you start poking around into your family's past. That's what Leila learned when she started dating Dave. She had no idea that he had a half-brother, or that his half-brother was in charge of a company that Dave wanted to take over. It was all a huge shock to her.

To make matters worse, Dave's extremely photogenic, suave, handsome, bronzed older half-brother Nash was none too pleased about the situation. He had killed the contract killer who was hired to take out Dave, and he was worried about the consequences that could come from it. It was a tense few weeks, but thankfully everything turned out okay in the end.

As you can imagine, Leila was shocked to find out that Dave had been betrayed by his own brother, who had hired a contract killer to take over the family business, Leaver Land Company. This was all in an effort to gain power over the company and ultimately, Dave. Nash had already started to divide the company and take control, using Meredith as an unwitting puppet. However, upon realizing what he had unleashed and just how severe his actions were, Nash opted to put an end to the chaos that he started by killing the contract killer himself.

Although this all was devastating for Dave, Leila's sex life with him has never been better. She attributes this phenomenon to Nash's actions as it has forced both of them closer together as they navigate their newfound family dynamics and figure out how living together is going to pan out. With so much newness being experienced; Leila feels more alive than ever before!

Dave's brother Nash had tried to right a wrong by killing the contract killer. Leila was full of mixed emotions upon finally learning this—she was angry and so incredibly sad that Dave's brother felt he had to take matters into his own hands, but also impressed by the sense of loyalty and family he seemed to have.

When Dave confronted Nash about it, Nash finally cracked and owned up to his mistake. He admitted what he had done and explained that he only wanted to protect Dave, despite the fact that they had relatively only just met. It was clear that Nash still cared deeply for him, and Leila respected that. After all, she loved and cared deeply for Dave as well and they also had just recently met face to face months ago. This moment showed her not only that Dave and Nash shared an incredible bond, but also how far she and Dave had come in their relationship — something she would never forget.

Although a seemingly surreal situation, Leila and Dave have found bliss in their relationship despite all the drama that surrounded them. Dave's loyalty to his family and his willingness to do anything for love, including giving up his pursuit of his brother's company, as his brother gave up the same pursuit of Leaver Land so his brother could have it, shows the strength of their connection and their dedication to each other. They did agree to put each other on the Board of Directors and profit Sharing with their respective companies and also after Meredith confessing to Dave her knowledge of Nash and siding with him, adding Meredith to Nash's Board.

Dave's capacity for love is something that Leila admires and finds extremely attractive. She has never been able to find such a strong connection with another man before Dave. In her eyes, he is the most heroic figure she has ever encountered - something she never expected to find in a man.

Thanks to Dave's selfless nature, Leila has experienced an entirely new level of satisfaction, both sexually and spiritually. In just a few short months, her life had changed more than she could ever have imagined - all due to the extreme measures taken by Dave in pursuit of their mutual bliss.

In the immediate end, love won. Dave and Leila were finally able to be together and live happily ever after, at least for now. Nash was able to start a new life with the knowledge that although he committed a grave sin against his Higher Power and humanity and would be in prison if he was not a wealthy businessman, he had made the right decision. Besides, the killer who he took out was a guy with purposely acid destroyed fingerprints due to making himself unidentifiable for a prolific lifetime of blackmailing, extortion and murderous crimes. Leila was finally able to have the best sex of her life with the man she loved.

After so much intensity, Leila and Dave decided to leave for a four day five night flight and cruise to Cozumel to re-energize.

Leila lay in Dave Anderson's arms, filled with pleasure and emotion. She had never felt so desired before - not even close to it! He looked into her eyes deeply as he caressed every part of her body tenderly; she could feel the electricity between them.

"You're driving me wild," Leila whispered breathlessly when their lips finally parted for a moment. "I've never met anyone like you."

Dave smiled mischievously, his jade green eyes alive with passion. "And I think you are the sexiest person I have ever known," he replied huskily, drawing her closer again and deepening the kiss until they were both lost in its intensity.

Leila couldn't help but be swept away by this incredible man who was slowly taking over all aspects of her life... yet at the same time she knew there were secrets lurking beneath his seductive exterior that frightened even him: dark things from his past that could destroy everything if revealed too soon or too harshly....

*****

Leila and Dave were locked in an intense embrace, their lips moving hungrily against one another. Leila's heart was pounding as she felt the strength of his arms around her body and heard him whisper he had never met anyone like her. She shivered with pleasure at his words; they sent electricity coursing through her veins.

She pulled back just enough to look into his eyes, a deep green that seemed so familiar even though it was only months ago the first time they'd seen each other that night at the club. She knows they were winning in love when he finally told her about his past dark secrets – which scared both of them badly but didn't crush feelings for each other instead reignited those old flames again making all things new and fresh between the two in lovebirds in the Cozumel villa nest over watching full moon light up this romantic moment happening here now - Leila spoke "what better way can be there? To end these series of moments together we shared! " Dave's past dark scares them both. But even as she tries to keep him at arm's length, she can't deny the intense attraction between them-or the fact that Dave seems determined to win her heart...

*****

"So what do you say, Leila? Will you marry me?" Dave asked, getting down on one knee and gazing up at her with love and adoration.

Leila was taken aback by the suddenness of it all, but she could see in his eyes that he was sincere. And she realized that she felt the same way about him. "Yes," she said softly, tears of happiness welling up in her eyes. "I will."

He slipped the huge trillion cut diamond ring onto her finger and then stood up to kiss her again; this time there was no holding back. They kissed passionately as their friends and family cheered them on - they knew this was just the beginning of a beautiful journey for these two souls who were meant to be together forever.

Leila then woke up from her Sterling wine induced deep sleep, in the villa master bedroom to relieve herself, crawling from under Dave's heavily muscled leg covering her right calf...

Grab a Glass of Wine if you partake,

Relax and Enjoy .

Prepare for the roller-coaster that will

continue!

.